Little Princesses

The Desert Princess

Little Princesses
The Desert Princess

By Katie Chase

Illustrated by Leighton Noyes

Red Fox

Special thanks to Narinder Dhami

THE DESERT PRINCESS
A RED FOX BOOK 978 0 099 48836 1 (from January 2007)
0 099 48836 1

First published in Great Britain by Red Fox,
an imprint of Random House Children's Books

This edition published 2006

3 5 7 9 10 8 6 4 2

Series created by Working Partners Ltd
Copyright © Working Partners Ltd, 2006
Illustrations copyright © Leighton Noyes, 2006
Cover illustration by Nila Aye

Papers used by Random House Children's Books are natural, recyclable products
made from wood grown in sustainable forests. The manufacturing processes conform
to the environmental regulations of the country of origin.

Set in 15/21pt Bembo Schoolbook

Red Fox Books are published by Random House Children's Books,
61–63 Uxbridge Road, London W5 5SA,
a division of The Random House Group Ltd,
in Australia by Random House Australia (Pty) Ltd,
20 Alfred Street, Milsons Point, Sydney, NSW 2061, Australia,
in New Zealand by Random House New Zealand Ltd,
18 Poland Road, Glenfield, Auckland 10, New Zealand,
and in South Africa by Random House (Pty) Ltd,
Isle of Houghton, Corner Boundary Road & Carse O'Gowrie,
Houghton 2198, South Africa

THE RANDOM HOUSE GROUP Limited Reg. No. 954009
www.kidsatrandomhouse.co.uk

A CIP catalogue record for this book is available from the British Library.

Printed and bound in Great Britain by
Cox & Wyman Ltd, Reading, Berkshire

For Teazle, who would be a
Little Princess – if she wasn't already Queen!
– A.J.C.

For Holly, my favourite goddaughter.
And for Laura, my other favourite
goddaughter
– L.N.

Chapter One

"Is it time to go yet, Dad?" Rosie asked, hurrying into the castle kitchen, where her father and her younger brother, Luke, were sitting at the enormous pine table. "I don't want to be late."

Her father laughed. "You asked me that five minutes ago!" he pointed out. "If we leave now, we'll be too early!"

"Sorry," Rosie said, and grinned. "I'm just so excited about Emma's party. Everyone at school's been talking about it."

"You look different," Luke said, staring at Rosie's costume. She wore a long, golden dress, a thin gold headband and armfuls of bangles.

"Mum made the dress from some bits of material we found in Great-aunt Rosamund's sewing room," Rosie explained.

Luke nodded wisely. "I know what you're dressed as," he said proudly. "An ancient eruption!"

Rosie and Mr Campbell burst out laughing.

"Nearly right!" Rosie said. "An ancient *Egyptian!*"

"Hasn't Emma's family just come back from Egypt?" asked Mr Campbell.

Rosie nodded. "Emma said they went on a boat trip down the River Nile and saw the Pyramids," she replied. "Emma loved it so much she wanted her birthday party to have an ancient Egyptian theme."

"That's a great idea," said Mr Campbell.

Rosie nodded. "And I was *really* pleased when Emma invited me because we haven't been friends for long."

Rosie and her family had left their own home several months ago to move into Great-aunt Rosamund's castle in Scotland. Great-aunt Rosamund, Rosie's favourite relative, loved travelling the world and collecting beautiful antiques to fill her home. She was now away for a couple of years on another trip, and she had asked Rosie's family to move in and look after the castle while she was gone.

"Can I see the invitation again?" Luke asked eagerly. "It had funny pictures on it!"

Rosie pulled a glossy cream card from the pocket of her dress and laid it on the table. All the details for the party were listed in bright gold lettering and then underneath

 it said, "Could all guests come as glittering ancient Egyptian princes and princesses?"

Around the edges of the invitation there were lots of ancient Egyptian drawings, including one of a pharaoh dressed in white and gold robes, with an elaborate headdress.

"What's that, Dad?" Rosie asked, pointing at a picture of a fabulous, cat-like beast. It had the body of a lion, a human head and large wings folded neatly against its sides.

"That's the Sphinx!" replied Mr Campbell. "He's a legendary beast, and there's an enormous stone statue of him in Egypt, next to the Pyramids."

"He looks grumpy," Luke remarked.

"He wasn't very friendly!" Mr Campbell

agreed. "According to the myths, the Sphinx would stop travellers who were passing and ask them to solve a riddle. If they failed, he would swallow them whole!"

"What's the riddle?" asked Rosie. "Does anyone know the answer?"

Mr Campbell nodded. "Oh, yes, it's very famous now." He smiled mysteriously at Rosie and Luke and set them the riddle. "What has four legs in the morning, two legs in the afternoon and three in the evening?"

Puzzled, Rosie and Luke stared at each other.

"It must be some kind of monster!" Luke guessed.

"Tell us, Dad!" said Rosie.

"The answer is 'a person'!" Mr Campbell said, chuckling at Rosie and Luke's surprised faces. "The riddle is called 'The Three Ages of Man'. When you're a baby, you crawl on all fours. That's the first age or 'morning' of your life. When you're an adult, you walk on—"

"Two legs!" Rosie interrupted.

"Exactly," Mr Campbell agreed. "And that's the second age, or the 'afternoon', of your life. And when you're old, you walk with a stick – that's three legs – and that's the 'evening' of your life!"

"That's hard!" Luke laughed. "I'd never have got that."

"You'd have ended up as the Sphinx's dinner!" Rosie told him.

Luke studied the Egyptian drawings carefully. "The people have got weird make-up on," he said.

"Oh!" Rosie clapped a hand to her mouth. "I knew there was something I'd forgotten! Mum said I could borrow some of her glittery eye-shadow."

"Don't trip over your dress!" called Mr
Campbell, as Rosie dashed out of the
kitchen. "We've got plenty of time."

Rosie picked up her skirt and
hurried up the main staircase next
to the Great Hall. Her parents'
bedroom was the biggest of
all the rooms on the second
floor. It had a four-poster
bed, draped with
pale-lilac curtains
patterned with
glittering blue and green
peacocks. Large windows looked out over the
hills and lake, and the walls were hung with
pictures collected by Great-aunt Rosamund
on her travels.

Rosie found the pot of eye-shadow on the
dressing table and began to apply it carefully.

When she'd finished, she stared at herself
in the mirror. Now I really do look like an
ancient Egyptian! she thought, tilting her
head this way and that. As she did so, her
gaze suddenly fell on a small picture hanging
beside the mirror. It was an ancient Egyptian
painting on papyrus.

"I can't believe I've never noticed that
before!" Rosie said to herself, taking a closer
look.

The picture showed a young girl, wearing
a white silk dress decorated with gold thread.
The girl's face was sad even though two cats,
one black and one ginger, sat at her feet,
their tails curled neatly round their bodies.
Rosie looked at the cats closely and noticed
that they looked rather unhappy too.

"It's another little princess!" Rosie gasped,
staring at the gold jewellery the girl was
wearing. "It *must* be!"

Great-aunt Rosamund's castle held an
amazing secret. There were little princesses
hidden everywhere! Rosie's great-aunt had
left her a secret note, warning Rosie to look
out for the princesses. Each time she found
one, Rosie was whisked away on a fantastic
adventure – and now, here was another!

Her heart thumping with excitement,
Rosie bobbed a curtsey. "Hello," she said,

just as her Great-
aunt Rosamund had
instructed in the note.

At once a warm
breeze streamed out
of the painting and
swirled around Rosie.
The breeze was heavy
with the smell of exotic
perfume, and it sparkled
with tiny grains of
golden sand. Rosie
closed her eyes as the
breeze grew stronger
and lifted her off her
feet. She knew that
she was about to find
herself in a magical
new land . . .

Chapter Two

A few seconds later, Rosie felt her feet touch the ground, and the breeze that had brought her died away. She could feel the heat of the sun on her face and hear the gentle lapping of water even before she opened her eyes. When she did open them, she found herself blinking in bright sunshine as she looked around eagerly.

"Oh!" Rosie gasped.

She was standing on the bank of a mighty river, and slender reeds swayed gently in the light breeze. In the distance she could see a dazzling white building surrounded by lush green gardens. Beyond that, a village of small

houses nestled in the shade of palm trees,
before the landscape changed into the bronze
sands of the desert, which stretched away in
every direction.

"Where am I?" Rosie said to herself.
Her dress billowed around her in a gust of
wind and she realized that her clothes had
changed. She now wore a long, pale-blue
robe and gold bands on her arms and ankles.
Curiously, Rosie put a hand to her head
and found that her hair was braided into

lots of thin plaits, sealed with
brightly coloured beads.

Just then, Rosie noticed
a girl kneeling on the
riverbank not far away.
Two cats, one black, one
ginger, sat quietly beside
her, their long tails waving.
Rosie's heart missed a

beat. I must be in ancient Egypt because that's the little princess from the painting, she thought excitedly. She looks sad – maybe I can help her! Determined to find out what was wrong, Rosie hurried over to the girl. As she drew nearer, the girl glanced up. She looked very surprised to see Rosie, and scrambled to her feet, scooping her cats up into her arms.

Now that she was closer, Rosie could see that the little princess's long black hair was intricately braided, and each plait was sealed with blue and gold beads. Like Rosie, the princess had gold bands around her wrists and ankles, but they were studded with blue gems. Her dark eyes were outlined with black, and the lids were covered with glittery green eye-shadow.

The girl stepped forward "I am Princess Aisha, daughter of Pharaoh Amenophis, and I welcome you to Egypt!" she said grandly. "But how did you get here?" she added curiously.

"I'm Rosie," Rosie replied, as the cats stared at her. The ginger one had brilliant emerald-green eyes while the black cat's shone like yellow topaz. "I came by magic!" she explained.

Princess Aisha looked very excited. "Magic!" she cried. "Of course! I asked the gods for help, and they've sent *you*!"

"I hope I can help," Rosie said sympathetically. "But I don't think I was sent by the gods. What's wrong?"

Princess Aisha's face fell. "Oh, Rosie, my oldest sister Nafretiri is very ill!" she explained in a trembling voice. "She has had a terrible fever for the past five days, and the priests say it is caused by an evil spirit trying to take Nafretiri to the Underworld before her time."

Rosie looked puzzled. "The Underworld?"

Aisha nodded. "Where the dead go," she whispered.

"That's terrible!" Rosie gasped. "Can't anyone make Nafretiri better?"

"My father has sent for Akori, the greatest magician in Egypt," Aisha went on. "He's with Nafretiri now, and very soon he'll tell us if she can be saved." She gave a deep sigh. "I came to our beloved River Nile to make a wish and ask the gods to save my sister and everyone in Egypt" – she looked hopefully at Rosie – "and then *you* appeared!"

"I'll do whatever I can to help," Rosie told Aisha. "But why do the people of Egypt need saving too?"

Aisha looked even more miserable.

"Because an ancient prophecy says that if the eldest daughter of the pharaoh passes away before her sixteenth birthday, then Egypt will fall to her greatest enemy, the Babylonians!" she replied.

"How old is Nafretiri?" asked Rosie.

"She is fifteen years old," Aisha sighed. "Which means that the prophecy could come true! And the Babylonians know of the prophecy, and know that Nafretiri is sick. So their forces are gathering on the borders of Egypt, ready to attack!"

Chapter Three

"Oh!" Rosie gasped. "How can we stop them?"

"Nafretiri must get well!" Aisha said firmly. "Egypt needs her to get better, and my parents and I cannot bear to lose her!" She stared hopefully at Rosie. "If you were sent here by magic, you must have great powers. Can you make my sister better?"

Regretfully Rosie shook her head. "I don't have any magic at all!" she explained. "I'm very sorry, Aisha. But I'll do anything else I can."

Aisha looked a little downcast. But then

she smiled. "Why don't you come to the palace with me?" she suggested. "Perhaps Akori will have good news about Nafretiri."

"I'd love to," Rosie said eagerly.

"Then you shall be my honoured guest!" Aisha replied. "Do you like cats, Rosie?"

Rosie nodded. Ever since she'd arrived, she'd been longing to stroke the two beautiful animals curled up in Aisha's arms.

"Here, take Kebi," Aisha said, handing the ginger cat to Rosie. "He's very friendly. So is Nebibi, but sometimes he's a little shy."

Happily Rosie took the ginger cat. Kebi stared up at her for a moment with his bright green eyes. Then he snuggled up against her, tucking his head under her chin.

A moment later, he began to purr, a deep throaty rumble.

"He likes you!" Aisha declared, beaming at Rosie as she led the way along the bank of the river.

"What do the cats' names mean?" asked Rosie.

"Kebi is 'Honey'," explained Aisha. "And Nebibi is 'Panther'."

Rosie grinned. "Their names really suit them," she said.

As they walked along the riverbank, Rosie realized that they were heading for the large white building she'd spotted earlier. Soon they were walking through lush gardens, dotted with tall trees and shady pools. Rosie was surprised to see that she recognized some of the plants from her own garden. There were white lilies, blue cornflowers and brightly coloured poppies. Pink water-lilies floated

in the pools, shaded by
apple and plum trees
and others laden
with figs and
olives.

"Everything's
so green!"
Rosie said,
looking
around.
"And yet
you're so
close to the
desert."

"It's because of our
great River Nile," replied Aisha.
"Every year it waters our fields and gardens.
Without it, we would not survive."

The palace was painted a pure snow-
white. Tall columns supported high ceilings,

and the enormous doors were a deep, rich blue. Rosie didn't know where to look first. Above her was a light blue ceiling painted with birds in flight. Under her feet was a floor of green glazed tiles painted with fish swimming amongst clusters of reeds. And the walls were painted with animals, embellished with jewels and gold.

"My father is in the audience chamber with his advisers and the priests," Aisha told Rosie. "This way."

She led Rosie along a wide corridor towards golden doors. Before they even reached the chamber, Rosie could hear the buzz of many voices. She soon saw that the room was packed, and she and Aisha had to slip in at the back. Aisha led Rosie to a couch, where they sat down among the soft cushions. Kebi and Nebibi immediately curled up on the girls' laps and went to sleep.

"That's my father," Aisha whispered to Rosie, pointing ahead of her.

Rosie looked and saw the pharaoh sitting on a magnificent golden throne at the front of the room. The throne was inlaid with precious stones, and its feet were carved in the shape of a lion's paws. Aisha's father wore flowing white robes and a regal headdress of blue and gold. He was surrounded by attendants, some of whom were fanning him with large palm leaves, but his face was anxious.

A loud *thudding* noise suddenly echoed along the corridor and through the room. Everyone in the room fell silent.

"What's that?" Rosie asked Aisha in a low voice.

"It's Akori, the magician," she replied. "That's the sound of his staff. He's coming from my sister's room to tell us how she is."

The next moment an elderly man swept into the room, staff in hand. His long blue cloak flared out behind him. As he approached the pharaoh, Rosie could see that a huge, blazing yellow sun was embroidered on the back of the cloak.

"Akori!" the pharaoh said, getting to his feet. "Tell me, good friend, how is my daughter? Will she recover?"

Akori stared solemnly at the pharaoh for a moment. Then, very slowly, he shook his grey head. Everyone in the chamber gasped with horror, and Rosie saw tears in Aisha's eyes. Quickly Rosie slid an arm around her friend.

"There is no hope for Princess Nafretiri,"

announced Akori sadly. "The fever is now very strong. We are going to lose our beloved princess, and I fear Egypt will fall to the Babylonians!"

Chapter Four

Rosie bit her lip and tried to comfort Aisha, who had begun to cry beside her. The pharaoh sank down onto his throne, looking pale and shaken.

"Rosie," Aisha said, suddenly looking very determined, "will you take Nebibi, please?"

Rosie nodded, wondering what Aisha was planning to do, as the princess placed the black cat on Rosie's lap next to Kebi.

"Great Akori!" Aisha called, stepping forward.

The magician whirled around to

look at her. "Yes, Princess?"

"You are wrong!" Aisha said in a clear, firm voice. "There *must* be a way to save my sister!"

Everyone in the chamber immediately turned to look at each other, muttering under their breath. Rosie could see that they were very shocked indeed that Aisha had spoken to the great magician in such a way. Determined to show support for her friend, she picked up both cats and hurried over to stand beside Aisha.

"Aisha!" The pharaoh had risen to his feet again. "You cannot speak to Akori in this way! Apologize at once!"

"No, Great Pharaoh." Akori raised his staff, and Rosie was relieved to see that the magician didn't look angry at all. "I am not offended. It is understandable that Princess Aisha is worried about her sister.

However" – Rosie felt her tummy turn over as Akori suddenly pointed his staff at her – "I *do* want to know who *you* are!"

"I'm Rosie," Rosie said bravely, "and I came here, to Egypt, by magic! My Great-aunt Rosamund told me how!"

Everyone, including Akori, looked amazed. But then, to Rosie's relief, the pharaoh stepped down from the platform and came towards her, smiling.

"My mother had a magic friend called Rosamund when she was a child," he said

thoughtfully. "She used to tell me stories about her. I believe that my mother's friend must have been your great-aunt!"

Rosie nodded as the pharaoh looked kindly at her.

"You are very welcome here, Rosie," he went on, "but I am sorry you could not have come at a happier time." He sighed deeply. "The Babylonians will attack as soon as they hear that Nafretiri cannot be saved. I must go and consult with my military advisers."

"But, Father——" Aisha began.

The pharaoh shook his head at her sadly. "Aisha, take your friend Rosie to the women's quarters," he said. "You will be safe there."

He kissed his daughter gently and then left the chamber, followed by all the courtiers. Soon nobody remained except Rosie, Aisha and Akori.

"Princess, your love for your sister is

strong," the magician said approvingly. "You have a brave spirit."

Rosie bent down and put Nebibi and Kebi on the floor. They had spotted a stray leaf drifting across the tiles and immediately scampered after it like kittens. Meanwhile, Rosie looked pleadingly at Akori. "Is there anything we can do to save Nafretiri?" she asked.

"If there is, you will know, for you are a great magician!" Aisha added.

Akori frowned and began to pace up and down the room, his face wrinkled in concentration. "No, it's ridiculous!" he muttered to himself. "It would be foolish even to mention it—"

"What?" Rosie asked eagerly. "Please tell us!"

Akori hesitated, but then he spoke. "There is said to be a magic potion made by Neith, the goddess of healing," he said slowly. "The potion wards off evil spirits and heals the sick. It is the only thing that can save Nafretiri now."

"Then we must find this potion!" Aisha declared.

The magician shook his head. "Nobody knows if the Potion of Neith really exists or if it is just a legend," he explained. "According to the myth, it is hidden in a secret cavern, and the only creature who knows the whereabouts of the cavern is the Sphinx."

"The Sphinx!" Rosie gasped, remembering the picture on her party invitation.

"But the Sphinx may not exist

either," Akori added quickly. "He is also a creature of legend. And if he *does* exist, he will never reveal where the cavern is unless you answer his riddle!"

That must be the riddle Dad told me! Rosie thought, as a servant came into the chamber.

"Great Akori, the pharaoh is asking for you," the attendant announced.

Akori smiled sadly at the girls. "I'm sorry there is nothing more I can do," he said quietly, and left.

Rosie glanced at her friend. She'd thought Aisha would be downcast by Akori's news, but the princess looked very excited.

"Rosie, my grandmother told me that the Sphinx *does* exist!" Aisha cried. "She said that he lives near the Pyramids. He only appears to those he wishes to see, but I *must* try to find him! I have to bring the magic potion back to Nafretiri." She frowned. "I only hope I can answer the riddle."

"That's why I'm coming with you, Aisha!" Rosie declared, a big smile on her face. "You see, I already *know* the answer to the Sphinx's riddle!"

Chapter Five

"You do?" Aisha said, in amazement. "What is it?"

Quickly, Rosie repeated the riddle her dad had told her — and its answer.

Aisha laughed. "I'd never have guessed!" she said.

"Well, we don't have to guess because we know the answer now," Rosie said cheekily. "All we have to do is find the Sphinx!"

Aisha nodded. "We'll have to get a boat up the Nile," she said. "But we must leave without being seen, or we won't be allowed out of the palace. Not with the Babylonians about to attack." Then she smiled. "Luckily, I know a sneaky way out behind the temple of Isis!" she whispered. "Follow me, Rosie. Come, Nebibi. Come, Kebi."

The girls went out of the chamber, and Nebibi and Kebi padded quickly after them, tails waving.

"We'll leave my cats in the garden of the women's quarters," Aisha explained as she hurried down a corridor to another part of the palace. "They can't come with us. It might be dangerous!"

The garden next to the women's quarters was enclosed by high sandstone walls. Aisha bent down and Nebibi and Kebi immediately ran lightly over to her.

"You must stay here, my darlings," she said gently, as the two cats curled themselves lovingly around her ankles. "Rosie and I will be back soon."

Then Aisha led Rosie back inside the palace. As they turned the

corner, Rosie glanced back and
saw that the cats were now chasing
brightly coloured butterflies among the
flowers.

"Don't worry," Aisha laughed, seeing
Rosie pause to watch the cats. "They never
catch them!"

Aisha stopped to collect an old hooded
cloak from the servants' quarters. "So the
boatmen don't recognize me," she told Rosie,
throwing it around her shoulders and pulling
the hood up to hide her face. Then she led
the way through a maze of corridors.

The palace was so huge that soon Rosie's
head was spinning. But at last Aisha brought
Rosie outside and into the temple gardens.
The Temple of Isis was a tall white building,
with two slender pillars at the front, both
carved with lotus flowers. It stood very close
to the River Nile.

"Follow me," Aisha whispered, leading Rosie to the back of the temple. A flight of white stone steps led down to a small gate right on the bank of the river. "Hardly anyone uses this exit except the Handmaidens of Isis when they want to make offerings to the river," the princess explained. "There's a guard on the gate, but he's always asleep!"

The two girls ran quietly down the steps to the gate. Just as Aisha had said, an elderly guard was sitting there on a bench, snoring softly. Aisha and Rosie slipped quietly through the gate and hurried along the riverbank.

"We must get a water-taxi," Aisha said. "It's the quickest way to the Pyramids.

Look, there are the boatmen just ahead of us."

Rosie saw a group of men sitting on the

riverbank, their sailboats bobbing on the
water.

"Kind friend," Aisha said to one, "will you
take us to the Pyramids?"

"The Pyramids?" The boatman stared at
Aisha in horror. "Don't you know that the
Babylonians are coming from that direction?"

"But we must go!" Rosie said pleadingly.

"I'll pay you well," Aisha added.

But the boatman shook his head. "You
won't find anyone willing to take you to
such a dangerous place," he said sternly, and
the others nodded in agreement.

Rosie looked around
anxiously for another
solution. A little way
off, she noticed a boy
sitting cross-legged
on a small wooden
boat near the bank.

"Let's try that boy," Rosie suggested to Aisha. "Maybe he'll take us."

The boatmen burst out laughing.

"In that tiny little boat?" one scoffed.

"You won't get far," another chuckled.

But the girls were already hurrying towards the boy.

"Hello!" Rosie called. "Could you take us to the Pyramids, please?"

The boy stared at the girls, shading his eyes from the sun. "The Babylonians are not far from the Pyramids!" he called back. "It is very dangerous! Are you sure you want to go there?"

"Yes, definitely," Rosie said.

"We'll pay whatever you ask!" promised Aisha. "*Please!*"

The boy hesitated. Then he shrugged. "Very well," he said slowly. Rosie and Aisha looked at each other with relief. "But I don't

want any money. In payment, you can
tell me why it is you are so eager to head
straight into danger!"

He jumped up and held out his hand to
help the girls aboard. Then he unfurled the
white sail, and began

to guide the little
boat up the
wide river.
"Thank
you!" Rosie
said gratefully.
"I'm Rosie and
this is Aisha. What's your name?"

"My name is Rami," the boy replied. "And
it is a pleasure to meet you both, Rosie and
Aish—" The boy's mouth fell open. "You
are the princess!" he gasped. "I thought I
recognized you from somewhere! We must
turn back immediately—"

"No!" Aisha said firmly. "We must get to the Pyramids before it is too late!"

Quickly Rosie told Rami how she'd come to Egypt and found both Nafretiri and the whole country in great danger. She explained that the magic Potion of Neith was the only thing that could save everyone.

"So we must find the Sphinx, Rami," Aisha added, as they sailed on up the Nile. "He will tell us where the potion is hidden."

Rami looked doubtful. "Many people come this way, seeking the Sphinx," he said. "Most never find him. Those that do must answer his riddle before he will help them."

"Is it true that those who can't answer are swallowed whole?" Rosie asked nervously. She glanced up at the sky. They had been sailing for a while now, and the sun was starting to set.

Rami laughed. "I think that only happens

when the Sphinx is in a very bad mood!"
he explained. "I've heard him purring a lot
recently, so you might be lucky."

Aisha stared at him. "You've heard the
Sphinx purring?" she asked.

Nodding, Rami pointed to the horizon.
"The Sphinx can be found where the sun
meets the sand," he told them. "Like any cat,
he loves to bask in the rays of the sun!" He
pulled in the sail a little, and the boat began
to slow. "Look, the sun is sinking there to
meet the sand." Rami said, pointing to the
setting sun, which was dipping between two

pyramids. "That is where you will find the Sphinx – if he wants you to."

Rami skilfully steered the boat into the bank. "I can't get any closer," he told the girls, helping them ashore. "You'll have to walk the rest of the way." He handed Rosie a leather flask. "Take this water. I'll wait here for you, but hurry. The desert is a dangerous place at night, Babylonians or not!"

"Thank you!" Aisha said gratefully.

She and Rosie waved at Rami, and then set off towards the desert. As they walked, the girls kept their eyes on the horizon, where

the sun was sinking towards the sand in a
haze of orange, pink and gold. They could
see the peaks of the Pyramids in the distance.

At first Rosie and Aisha walked quickly,
but once they reached the desert, they were
forced to slow down. The golden sand was
soft and deep, making it very difficult
to walk.

Eventually they reached the top
of a particularly high sand dune.
"Aisha, look!" Rosie cried,
pointing down at the desert
in front of her. The sand was
aglow with the light of
the setting sun as it sank
between the Pyramids.
"See how the sun is
sinking into the
sand right
there?"

Rosie gasped. "We've made it, Aisha!"

Aisha grinned and the two girls ran down the sand dune excitedly.

"Where's the Sphinx?" Aisha asked, spinning round to look in every direction.

"I don't know," Rosie replied, suddenly feeling disappointed. All she could see was the Pyramids, dunes and sand.

Exhausted, Aisha sat down and leaned back against a nearby sandy ridge. "Maybe we've missed him," she said miserably.

"Have a drink," Rosie suggested, sitting down next to her friend and passing her the flask.

The girls shared the water between them, in a dejected silence.

Then, suddenly, Rosie heard a low rumbling sound. "What's that?" she began.

But before Aisha could reply, both girls cried out as a fine shower of sand rained down over them.

"The ridge!" Aisha cried, jumping to her feet. "It's moving!"

Hardly able to believe her eyes, Rosie stared at the ridge as the two girls backed away. It was trembling and shifting as if it was alive! "Is it an earthquake?" Rosie gasped.

Aisha clapped a hand to her mouth, her eyes round. Clutching Rosie's arm, she pointed upwards.

Rosie looked up. To her utter amazement, the Sphinx himself towered over her. He

had
the
face
of a man,
surrounded by
the distinctive headdress of a
pharaoh, but he also had wings and
the furry body of a lion, complete with a
shaggy golden mane and a long tail.

The Sphinx opened his brilliant emerald-green eyes and blinked, as if he'd just woken up from a long sleep. "Now, perhaps you'd like to explain why you were sitting on my paw?" he roared.

Chapter Six

Rosie was so shocked she couldn't speak.
Neither could Aisha. The girls backed away a
little, gazing up at the huge beast in front of
them.

The Sphinx stretched and then took a step
towards the friends. Rosie and Aisha gasped
as they felt the ground shake beneath them.

"Well?" the Sphinx growled, glaring at
them.

"Mighty Sphinx!" Aisha began, but the
Sphinx couldn't hear her.

He yawned, showing large white teeth.
"I'm waiting!" he growled.

"MIGHTY SPHINX!" Aisha shouted as

loudly as she could, but still the Sphinx took

no notice.

"He can't hear us,"
Rosie told Aisha.
"Let's climb up that
sandbank over there
and then we'll be level
with his ears!"

The two girls ran over to the
sandbank and scrambled up it as quickly as
they could. Meanwhile the Sphinx shook his
headdress and looked around.

"Where have you gone?" he snapped. "I'm
not finished with you yet!"

"We're here, Mighty Sphinx!" Aisha called
from the top of the sandbank.

Rosie tried not to feel scared as the Sphinx
slowly turned his enormous head to stare at
them.

"Explain why you have disturbed my

sleep!" the Sphinx demanded. "Do you know how annoying it was to find you sitting on my paw? You are like two little mosquitoes!"

"Please forgive us, Great Sphinx!" Rosie said breathlessly.

"We have come to find you because we have been told you are the wisest creature on earth!" added Aisha.

The Sphinx looked a little less angry and nodded his massive head, showering Rosie and Aisha with sand. "That is true," he said slowly. "But why are you here?"

"I need to find the Potion of Neith for my sister Nafretiri," Aisha explained. "Without it she will die!"

The Sphinx lifted his long tail and waved it lazily. "And why should I care?" he asked coldly.

"Because if we don't save Nafretiri, Egypt will fall to the Babylonians!" Rosie told him.

The Sphinx looked extremely bored. "Ah, yes, the prophecy," he said with another yawn. "I know all about that. After all, I made it!" Then he frowned. "Although I didn't expect the fall of Egypt to come *quite* so quickly. It feels as though it's happened rather too soon—"

"But it doesn't *have* to happen at all," Aisha broke in eagerly. "If you tell me where the potion is, my sister will be saved and there will be no war. The Babylonians will retreat

once they know that Nafretiri is well again."
The Sphinx raised his giant left paw and
stroked his chin. "Well," he said thoughtfully,
"it *would* be very troublesome for
me to have to get to know
the Babylonians. They'd
be bound to come and
pester me, and ask me
to tell their fortunes
and make more
prophecies."

"And if there
was a war," put
in Rosie, "all the
fighting would
disturb your sleep
too."

"Very true," the Sphinx
agreed. He looked at Aisha. "I know that you
have always been kind to cats," he went on

with a smile, "so I will help you."

Rosie and Aisha glanced at each other in delight.

"However," the Sphinx added gravely, "I will only tell you how to find the potion if you first prove yourselves worthy to enter the Cavern of Geb, God of the Earth, for that is where the potion lies hidden."

"Tell us how," begged Aisha.

The Sphinx shook his head. "You must answer my riddle," he replied.

Rosie tried not to smile at Aisha. She didn't want the Sphinx to realize that she already *knew* the answer to his riddle! "Please, tell us the riddle," Rosie said eagerly.

The Sphinx frowned, lifted his left paw and scratched his head. "Hmm . . ." he muttered. "As you are here to try and save Princess Aisha's sister, I will give you a riddle about two sisters!"

Rosie's mouth dropped open in shock. "Two sisters?" she gasped. "What about 'The Three Ages of Man'?"

The Sphinx laughed so hard that the sandbank beneath the girls' feet trembled. "That old chestnut?" he spluttered, still chuckling. "I haven't used that in years!"

Chapter Seven

Rosie was horrified. Glancing at Aisha, she saw that her friend's face had gone pale with shock and she felt horribly guilty. Rosie had been so sure she'd know the answer to the riddle. How would they ever get hold of the magic potion now?

"Don't worry, Rosie," Aisha whispered, patting her arm. "We still have a chance of answering this new riddle."

Rosie didn't feel too hopeful, but she managed a smile.

"Here is my riddle," the Sphinx announced grandly. "Two girls are born on the same day of the same month in the same year to

the same parents, and yet they are not twins.
How can this be?"

Rosie and Aisha stared at each other.

"That's not possible, is it?" Aisha whispered

Rosie. "If they are born on
the same day to the same
parents, they must be
twins!"

Rosie nodded, racking
her brains. There had been
a set of twins back at her old
school, and they had definitely
been born on the same day. It simply wasn't
possible that two babies born at the same
time, with the same mum and dad, *weren't*
twins! It had to be some kind of trick
question . . .

The girls looked at each other, bewildered.
Then, suddenly, Rosie gave a little gasp.
She remembered talking to Luke just after

they'd both started at their new school in the
village. Luke had been telling her about two
sisters in his class called Anna and Nina.

They had been born on the same day and
they had the same parents, but they weren't
twins because they had a sister of the same
age in another class, called Lana. They were
triplets!

Rosie bit her lip nervously.
Could that be the answer to
the riddle?

The Sphinx was swishing his
tail impatiently from side to side,
stirring up the sand. "Do hurry up,"
he muttered crossly. "I want to get
back to sleep, because things
are going to get very
noisy when

the Babylonians turn up!"

"I don't know what the answer is," Aisha whispered desperately to Rosie. "Do you?"

Rosie decided to give her idea a try. "The two sisters are part of a set of triplets," she said firmly, her heart pounding. "That's why they aren't twins!"

"Oh!" Aisha gasped, her face lighting up.

The Sphinx looked shocked for a moment. Then he smiled and nodded his head. "You are right!" he purred.

Aisha gave Rosie a big hug.

"Now I must keep my part of the bargain," the Sphinx went on, "and tell you where the Cavern of Geb is located."

"Is it far?" Rosie asked, her knees still trembling with relief.

The Sphinx threw his head back and laughed loudly, the sound echoing around the sand dunes. "Not at all," he replied. "In fact, it's right here!" The Sphinx lifted his right paw, and Rosie and Aisha were amazed to see a huge chasm in the desert sand beneath it. They could also see white stone steps leading down into the rift.

"Now listen carefully: the Cavern of Geb is at the bottom of these steps," the Sphinx said. "It is filled with fantastic magical treasures and glittering gems. The Potion of Neith is amongst them."

"How will we find it?" Rosie broke in.

The Sphinx flicked his tail impatiently. "You just *will*," he snapped. "But if you try to take anything else from the cavern – anything except the potion – then you will be destroyed by the gods!"

"We won't take anything," Rosie promised.

"Oh, and there is one more thing," the Sphinx went on, yawning now. "As soon as you touch the potion, the chasm will start to close. Sand will pour in, filling the hole. You will need to get out as fast as you can, if you hope to survive!"

Chapter Eight

Rosie gulped and glanced at Aisha, who was looking determinedly at the mouth of the chasm.

"Rosie, you wait here and I'll go into the cavern alone—" Aisha began.

"No way!" Rosie interrupted firmly. "I'm coming with you."

"Well, I must be going," the Sphinx said with a shiver. "It's getting rather chilly now the sun has gone down." He glanced up at the sky, which was turning a dusky dark blue, and then back at the girls. "Good luck and goodbye."

With one swift movement, the Sphinx unfolded his enormous wings and soared up

into
the
sky.
The girls
covered
their faces
as sand flew
everywhere.
Then they shook
the sand from
their clothes
and watched as
the Sphinx climbed
higher into the sky
towards the stars,
which were

starting
to glimmer here
and there.

"Let's go," Rosie said. "There's
no time to lose!"

Quickly the girls climbed down from
the sandbank and hurried over to the steps
which led into the chasm. Rosie had been
worried that it would be too dark for them
to find their way, so she was delighted to see
that the stairs were lit with dazzling diamond
torches fixed to the walls.

The girls hurried down the steps, going
deeper and deeper into the chasm. Suddenly

Aisha gasped with fright. "Look!"

Rosie's heart missed a beat. At the side of the steps lay a gleaming white skeleton, holding a sword in its bony hand.

"It must be someone who got trapped here trying to get out," Aisha whispered. Rosie nodded and shuddered.

The two girls hurried past the skeleton and on

down the stairs. The steps seemed to go on
for ever. Rosie was just wondering if they
would ever reach the cavern when suddenly
the steps came to an abrupt halt. They had
reached the entrance to a large cave.

Cautiously the girls made their way inside,
following a short tunnel which soon emerged
into an enormous chamber. As the girls
stepped into the chamber, they both stopped
dead and gasped in utter amazement.

"Oh, Rosie!" Aisha whispered. "Have you
ever seen anything so beautiful?"

Rosie was so mesmerized by the sight
in front of her that she couldn't reply. The
Cavern of Geb was a dazzling treasure trove.
Glittering in the torchlight were necklaces
and bangles made of gold and rubies and
pearls. Golden armour, inlaid with silver
and precious gems, glittered beside swords
with blades that seemed to be made of pure

diamond. Heaps of sparkling jewels – rubies,
emeralds, sapphires and amethysts – were
piled carelessly here and there on the floor,
and elaborate mirrors, goblets and treasure
chests were heaped up around the rocky
walls of the cavern.

Rosie and Aisha couldn't drag their eyes
away from the glittering treasures. Rosie felt
almost hypnotized as she stared at the intense
colours of the jewels. She knew she should be
looking for the Potion of Neith, but somehow
she just couldn't tear herself away.

Meanwhile Aisha knelt down before a pile
of sapphires that shimmered and shone in
every shade of blue imaginable. "There are so
many," she murmured. "Surely it wouldn't be
greedy to take just one . . ."

Rosie's gaze fell on a bottle standing alone
on a shelf just in front of her. The bottle was
made of translucent purple glass and it was

full of a liquid.

"The Potion of
Neith!" Rosie gasped,
shaking herself out of
her dazed state. She
looked over to Aisha
and saw to her horror
that the princess was
about to pick up one
of the sapphires.

"Aisha! Stop!"
Rosie yelled. She
ran over to
her friend and
pulled her to her
feet.

Aisha shook
her head, looking
as if she'd just
been woken from

a long sleep. "Thank you, Rosie!" she gasped. "I don't know what came over me."

"I think I've found the potion," Rosie told her urgently, leading Aisha over to it. "I'm sure this is it!"

Aisha stared at the purple bottle. "You're right," she agreed.

"Do you remember what the Sphinx told us?" Rosie said. "We've got to grab it and run for our lives!"

"I'm ready," Aisha murmured, her eyes fixed on the bottle.

"You grab the potion when I've counted to three, Aisha," Rosie said, her heart thumping. "One. Two. THREE!"

Aisha reached out and picked up the bottle. Immediately, there was a rumbling sound and the ground began to shake.

"The chasm's starting to close!" Rosie cried, as the treasures in the cavern began to tumble to the floor. "Hurry, Aisha! We have to get out of here!"

Chapter Nine

The girls ran towards the entrance of the cavern as precious gems showered down around them like glittering hailstones. But when they reached the stairs up out of the chasm, they were horrified to see that the desert sands were pouring in through the rift like fast-flowing water.

"Quick, Rosie!" Aisha shouted. "Look, the lower steps are already covered with sand."

The two girls waded through the sand and began racing up the stairs. It was hard work because they had to avoid the sand pouring down towards them. Behind them the level of the sand was rising at a frightening rate. Rosie knew that if they didn't keep climbing as fast as they could, they would soon be buried alive. She was panting so hard she thought her lungs would burst. Would the stairs never end?

But then Rosie saw the inky-blue darkness of the desert sky just above her. "Aisha!" she panted joyfully. "We're nearly there!"

Aisha was too exhausted to speak. With one final effort the girls reached the top of the steps and flung themselves out of the chasm. As they dashed to safety behind the nearest sand dune, there was an ear-splitting CRASH and the chasm closed up completely. Now it looked just like a normal part of the desert again, as if nothing extraordinary had ever been there.

"We made it, Aisha!" Rosie gasped, giving her friend a big hug.

"I couldn't have done it without you, Rosie!" Aisha said gratefully, gazing at the purple bottle she was still clutching. "But now we must take this potion to Nafretiri. I just hope we're not too late."

Although they were tired out, the girls hurried back to the river as fast as they could.

Rami was standing on his boat in the moonlight, anxiously looking out for them.

"I'm glad you're safe!" he said happily, helping them both aboard. He spotted the bottle in Aisha's hand. "And you have the potion! I guess you found the Sphinx then."

Rosie nodded. "We'll tell you all about it!" she said.

"Let me set sail first," Rami replied, glancing up at the sky. "The Sphinx is restless tonight. He is whipping up a sandstorm! We must return to the palace before it gets too windy to sail down the Nile."

As the little boat sped down the river, ahead of the storm, Rosie and Aisha told Rami the story of how they'd found the Potion of Neith.

Rami listened wide-eyed to their exciting tale. "You are both very brave!" he said admiringly as they finally reached the palace. "I'm proud that I was able to help."

"Thank you very much," Rosie said

warmly as
Rami brought
the boat close
to the riverbank.
"We would never
have made it without
you!"

"Rosie's right." Aisha slid one
of the heavy gold bangles from her
arm and held it out to the boy. "Please take
this in payment."

Rami shook his head. "It's much too
valuable—" he began.

"You may have helped to save my sister

and all of Egypt!" Aisha broke in. "Please take it."

Reluctantly Rami took the bracelet. "Thank you, Princess," he murmured shyly, beaming at her. "I'll be able to buy a new and bigger boat! But the *real* gift you and Rosie have given me is that I am part of your story."

Rosie and Aisha jumped ashore and waved as Rami set sail for home. Then they raced over to the palace. This time Aisha led Rosie towards the main entrance. It was heavily guarded. Six of the pharaoh's soldiers stood outside, swords drawn.

"Princess Aisha!" the Captain of the Guard exclaimed when he saw her. "What are you doing outside the palace walls? Nobody is meant to leave the palace with the Babylonians about to attack!"

Aisha assured him that she and Rosie were

completely safe, but she didn't have time to explain further. The girls hurried past the guards and through the palace to the women's quarters.

"This is Nafretiri's room," Aisha whispered, pushing open a set of red doors.

The room was in semi-darkness. Only a single oil lamp burned near the ornate, gilded bed. Rosie tiptoed across the room behind Aisha and stared down at Nafretiri, who was in a deep sleep. She looked very like Aisha, but her skin was flushed and her breathing sounded laboured. Rosie could see at a glance that she was very ill.

Scattered on the floor around the bed were strange blue stones which seemed to pulse with an inner light. Rosie stared at them curiously.

"They are lapis lazuli," Aisha whispered. "Gemstones that help to heal the sick."

A sound behind them made the girls turn

round. A tall and beautiful woman in a white robe had just glided quietly into the room.

"This is my mother," Aisha told Rosie.

The pharaoh's wife came over to the bed. "Aisha, my dear," she said softly, "the stones, Akori's magic, everything has failed." She sighed deeply and tears appeared in her eyes. "I fear our beloved Nafretiri is already on her journey to the Underworld!"

"No!" Aisha whispered fiercely. Rosie watched as her friend quickly uncorked the purple bottle and bent over the bed to put it to Nafretiri's lips. A little of the precious turquoise potion trickled into Nafretiri's mouth.

"What is that?" asked the queen.

"The Potion of Neith," Rosie replied. "Akori said it can heal the sick."

Aisha, Rosie and the queen watched hopefully for any sign of recovery in Nafretiri. But the princess lay there quiet and unmoving.

Rosie bit her lip to hold back her tears. It looked as though she and Aisha were too late after all.

Chapter Ten

"It doesn't work!" Aisha whispered. She turned away with a sob and Rosie went to comfort her. They had done their best, but it was no good . . .

But then the queen gasped. "Her eyes are opening!" she murmured. "Look!"

Rosie and Aisha turned back to see Nafretiri's long black lashes flutter open.

She looked up at them and yawned. Then she sat up, a smile on her lips. "Oh, I've had such a good sleep!" she sighed. "And so many wonderful dreams!"

"Praise be to the gods!" the queen cried, clasping her hands as Rosie and Aisha beamed at each other. "My daughter is cured!"

The doors were flung open as servants and attendants crowded into the room to see for themselves.

"How do you feel?" Aisha asked anxiously.

"Wonderfully refreshed!" Nafretiri replied. She looked from Aisha to Rosie with a grateful smile. "And while I was asleep, I saw your whole adventure in my dreams!"

Rosie and Aisha gasped in amazement.

"I thank you both a thousand times for saving me. But now I must go and speak with my father," Nafretiri went on, pushing back the covers.

The servants gathered round to help Nafretiri, but the queen waved them away. "We shall be your servants, Nafretiri!" she said.

Quickly Rosie and Aisha helped Nafretiri to dress in a blue robe, while the queen combed her daughter's long black hair. Then they all set off to find the pharaoh, who was still shut up with Akori and his military advisers.

Nafretiri went into the chamber first, and Rosie, who was behind her, saw the pharaoh start up from his chair, his face as white as if he had seen a ghost.

"My daughter!" he gasped in a faltering voice. "Is this your spirit, come to tell me that you are gone to the Underworld?"

"No, Father!" Nafretiri laughed. "It is really me! I am well again, thanks to Rosie and Aisha. They went on a dangerous adventure to find the magic Potion of Neith, and it has cured me! Father, they even spoke to the Sphinx himself!"

There was a gasp from the people in the room, and for a moment the pharaoh looked as if he couldn't quite believe it. But then, beaming, he rushed across the room to hug his daughter.

"The Potion of Neith?" Akori repeated. "So you and your friend found it after all, Princess Aisha!"

The pharaoh turned to Rosie and Aisha.

He was trying to look stern, but a smile
was playing around his lips. "I don't know
whether to praise or punish you!" he said.
"It was very dangerous to leave
the palace with the
Babylonians
preparing to
attack."

Before anyone
could reply, the
sound of running
footsteps was heard in
the corridor outside
and the doors of
the chamber were
thrown open. The
next moment, the
servants ushered in
a bedraggled and
windswept man

covered in sand.

"Great Pharaoh!" he gasped. "The commander of your troops on the border has sent me with urgent news! The Babylonians have been driven back into their own country by a mighty sandstorm!" He took a deep breath. "Egypt is saved!"

Rosie looked over at Aisha in delight as everyone in the room began to rejoice.

"We're safe!" Aisha gasped, hugging Rosie tightly.

"I'm so glad," Rosie said happily.

"Tonight we will have the greatest celebration Egypt has ever seen!" the pharaoh announced in delight. "Servants, send word to everyone in the palace to prepare for a huge feast!"

The chamber echoed with cheers and shouts of joy as the servants rushed to do his bidding.

Meanwhile, the pharaoh turned and smiled kindly at Rosie. "Without you, my country would be lost, as well as my beloved daughter," he said. "I owe you so much, Rosie. Will you stay for the party?"

"Thank you, Pharaoh," Rosie replied with a smile. "But I think I'd better get home. I have my own party to go to!"

"Very well." The pharaoh took her hand and held it for a moment. "But remember, my dear, that you will always be an honoured guest here in Egypt!"

"Goodbye, Rosie," Nafretiri said, hugging Rosie warmly.

"Thank you again," added the queen, embracing Rosie as well.

"Come and say goodbye to Kebi and Nebibi," said Aisha, leading Rosie out into the garden.

As soon as they saw the girls, the cats rushed over and rubbed against their legs. Rosie bent down to stroke them both.

"Say a very special goodbye to Rosie," Aisha said, sweeping the two cats up into her arms, "because she's a very special friend! And make her promise to visit us again soon."

"I will!" Rosie laughed. She stroked both cats, and they gently rubbed their heads against her cheek.

"Thank you, Rosie," Aisha said

gratefully. "I will never forget what you have done for me, for my family and for Egypt!"

Rosie hugged her. "Goodbye, Aisha! Goodbye, Nebibi and Kebi!"

As soon as she spoke, Rosie felt the familiar, scented whirlwind whip up around her and lift her off the ground. She caught a last glimpse of Aisha holding her purring cats before she closed her eyes . . .

A moment later she was back in her parents' bedroom in Great-aunt Rosamund's castle. Rosie blinked and then stared closely at the papyrus painting. She was thrilled to see that Aisha looked happy now. And Nebibi and Kebi looked more cheerful, too. Instead of sitting glumly at Aisha's feet, they were now playfully chasing butterflies.

"Rosie!" Rosie heard her dad call from downstairs. "Time to go."

"Coming!" Rosie replied and hurried out

of the room smiling to herself. She was going to enjoy the party even more now that she'd visited the *real* ancient Egypt!

THE END

Did you enjoy reading about Rosie's
adventures with the Desert Princess?
If you did, you'll love the next
Little Princesses
book!

Turn over to read the first chapter of
The Lullaby Princess.

Chapter One

Rosie sat on the floor of the castle's big bathroom rummaging through a deep cardboard box filled with smooth pebbles and pretty seashells. She began to pick out a handful of cowrie shells with glossy white sides. They were all different sizes, some so tiny they were hardly bigger than her fingernail, others large enough to cover the palm of her hand.

Her five-year-old brother, Luke, was lying on the floor next to her, stacking some large flat pebbles from the box into a pile. "Look at my tower, Rosie!" he said proudly.

Rosie rolled the cowrie shells in her hands. She had found the cardboard box at the bottom of one of the bathroom cupboards that morning while she had been helping her mum tidy up. Mrs Campbell had said that she could make a display on the bathroom shelf using the pebbles and shells.

Lifting the largest shell to her ear, Rosie listened to the soft swirling sound of the sea. It made her think of sandy beaches and blue skies. Holidays, Rosie thought longingly, as she stood up to place the shell on the shelf.

She glanced out of the bathroom window at the grey misty mountains of the Scottish Highlands and sighed. She loved living here but right now she couldn't help thinking it would be wonderful to be on a warm, sunny beach or swimming in the sea.

She arranged the shells on the shelf and then headed back to the old box. As she reached inside it, the sleeve of her jumper rubbed some of the dust off the top, and she saw the word *Hawaii* written in her Great-aunt Rosamund's loopy handwriting. Rosie knew that Hawaii was a tropical island far away and guessed that her adventurous great-aunt had once visited it and collected the shells and pebbles there.

I hope I find another little princess soon, Rosie thought as she bent down to look in the box again. She wanted a large shell for the centre of the display now. She was sure she could feel one, wrapped up in tissue paper right at the bottom of the box. Rosie pulled the package out and carefully began to peel away the layers of thin paper. She was right. There *was* a shell inside the tissue paper and it was beautiful. It was a spiral shape with a creamy outside and a glossy, pale pink interior. It was perfect for the display.

"Rosie! Luke!" their mum called up the stairs. "Lunch time!"

"Coming!" Luke shouted eagerly. He let his pebble tower fall to the floor with a crash and ran to the door.

Rosie was about to put the shell down and follow him when she noticed something interesting. The shiny pink inside of the shell had a picture drawn in black paint on it.

She stopped and looked more closely.

In the background of the drawing was a mountain that seemed to have smoke coming from the top of it. Rosie guessed that it must be a volcano. At the front of the picture, a girl was standing beside a canoe, looking anxiously at the volcano. She had long hair down to her waist, a skirt that looked like it was made of dried grass, and necklaces and anklets made of feathers and shells. On her head was a circular headdress of flowers. She looked very beautiful, but also very sad.

Rosie's heart started to beat faster with excitement. She felt sure this was another little princess, but there was only one way to find out.

She put the shell down on the shelf and dropped into a curtsey. "Hello," she whispered, staring intently at the girl in the picture.

Immediately, a breeze seemed to blow out of the shell. It filled the bathroom with

the scent of sweet flowers, pineapples and coconuts.

Rosie gasped as the breeze began to swirl around her, faster and faster. Drops of seawater seemed to be caught up in the air, glittering like bright crystals. She felt herself being lifted up, and she gasped and closed her eyes; she was going on another adventure!

A few moments later, Rosie felt herself being set gently down.

There was the smell of salt in the air and the feeling of warmth on her skin. Opening her eyes, Rosie saw that she was now sitting in a wooden canoe on a beach of sparkling white sand!

Rosie shifted on the seat of the canoe and heard the crackle of dried grass as she did so. She looked down to see that she was wearing a grass skirt dyed a deep pinky-red colour. A garland of yellow and white flowers hung around her neck, and putting a hand to her head, Rosie could feel a wreath of flowers surrounding her red-brown curls.

Suddenly Rosie heard someone puffing in exertion and felt the canoe move a little in the sand. She turned round. A girl with smooth brown skin and glossy, waist-length dark hair was trying to push the canoe. Her head was bent and she hadn't seen Rosie. Rosie caught her breath in surprise.

The girl glanced up. Seeing someone sitting in her canoe, she stopped quite still and stared at Rosie in amazement. She was wearing a purple grass skirt and necklaces and anklets made of pink flowers, shells and twinkling crystals. Over one shoulder hung a light brown bag which had tiny, rainbow-coloured shells sewn all over it in rows. Rosie recognized the girl as the little princess from the picture painted on the shell in the bathroom.

"Who are you?" asked the astonished princess.

Read the rest of *The Lullaby Princess* to follow Rosie's adventures!